TRULY MONS

WEREWOLVES

TRULY MONSTROUS TALES

WEREWOLVES

Peter Hepplewhite & Neil Tonge

Illustrated by David Wyatt

Hodder
Children's
Books

a division of Hodder Headline plc

Published by Hodder Children's Books 1999

Design by Linda Reed & Associates

10 9 8 7 6 5 4 3 2 1

A catalogue record for this book is available from the British Library

ISBN 0 340 73993 2

Printed and bound in Great Britain by The Guernsey Press Company Limited, Guernsey, C.I.

Hodder Children's Books
a division of Hodder Headline plc
338 Euston Road
London NW1 3B7

Contents

Contents

Introduction

Do you ever feel uncomfortable inside your skin, as if you know you should be faster and stronger? Do your hairy eyebrows meet in the middle of your forehead? When the moon is full do you feel restless, pacing the room from wall to wall? Watch out, you may be a werewolf.

"That's great," you think. "Imagine the people I can scare and I'll never have to hire a fancy dress costume in my entire life!" But don't be too sure you would enjoy yourself. Most werewolves ended up dead or locked up in hospitals.

So what is a werewolf? Forget Hollywood – as usual the movie-makers got it wrong. The film that set the pattern for other movies was *The Wolf Man* (1941), starring Lon Chaney Jnr. The werewolf of the cinema is a hairy monster that walks on two legs, more man than beast. The scriptwriters made it up and ignored the evidence of legend, folklore and history.

Another word for werewolf is 'lycanthrope'. It comes from the Greek words for wolf, *lykos*, and man, *anthropos*. At its simplest, it means a person who transforms into a wolf, perhaps with the help of evil magic. The shape-shifter becomes a real wolf, not a half-human cross-breed. Their feet and hands turn into paws, their arms are transformed into legs, only their eyes keep a spark of humanity. That is the stuff of fearsome legends.

A second meaning is sadder, and more real. A lycanthrope is someone who believes that they are a wolf, and behaves like one. One thousand three hundred years ago, the Greek doctor Paulus Aegineta described patients suffering from lycanthropy. Pitifully they wandered about

at night, howling when the moon rose, before scampering off to hide in graveyards. Their legs and hands were sore and bleeding from walking on all fours. In medieval Europe thousands of such sad, insane people were executed as witches and sorcerers.

But why has the idea of 'werewolves' gripped the human mind, more than any other kind of shape-shifting? (Well, were-sheep just doesn't sound the same!) The answer probably lies in prehistoric history. When early humans had to hunt for survival, wolves were their deadly rivals. This fear was passed down for countless generations and has never gone away. Even today, wolves are feared most where packs still run free.

Now, dare you turn the page, to meet the terror in *Truly Monstrous Tales: Werewolves*? Inside you'll find adventures to set you howling. Spin through time – from the werewolf horrors of Ancient Rome, to the twentieth century, when humans may be forced to admit that real wolves are not so bad after all.

Peter and Neil

The Werewolf of Ancient Rome

Werewolf stories are incredibly old. Even older than your granny. One of the most famous was written in the first century AD by the Roman author, Petronius Arbiter. Very little is known about him, except that he was in charge of entertainment at the court of the mad and bad Emperor, Nero. Life in the imperial court was full of plots and dangers so Arbiter always took care to seem relaxed, as if he were too laid-back to be a threat to anyone. However, he enjoyed poking fun at those around him and this made him powerful enemies. His death was messy, but we'll come to that later! Arbiter's creepy werewolf yarn is found in his novel, the *Satyricon*. It's still popular, very rude, and has been made into a film, but your parents probably wouldn't let you watch it.

One of the main characters in the *Satyricon* is the freed slave, Trimalchio. He has made a success of his life and to show off his wealth is holding a lavish banquet for his friends. After they have eaten, Trimalchio asks Niceros, another ex-slave, to tell a story. In the best horror tradition Niceros' adventure begins as the sun sets:

A Moonlit Walk

My master Gaius was on a business trip to Capua, so I thought while he was away from the house I'd take the opportunity to go and see my girlfriend, the gorgeous Melissa. I'm sure you've all done the same. If the cat is away the mice can play.

Since it was going to be a night walk I asked a guest in our house to come with me as far as the fifth milestone. He was a

soldier and as brave as hell. Very handy for scaring off robbers. We set off at sunset and before long the moon had risen. It was very bright, almost like being out at noon. We were on the main road, with the gravestones on either side of it. [In those days, tombstones lined the sides of the roads in southern Italy.]

After a brisk walk we stopped for a break. I spent some time counting how many gravestones I could see, then began thinking about how I was going to enjoy my night out with Melissa. I was relaxed and happy and wasn't worried about the soldier. I'd seen him reading inscriptions on the tombstones and when I lost sight of him I assumed that he had gone off somewhere to relieve himself.

A Werewolf on the Loose

A little while later I looked round to see what the soldier was up to, and by the gods, my heart leaped into my mouth. He had taken off all his clothes and there he was – stark naked. Weirdly, he'd piled his clothes into a heap at the side of the road and was peeing in a circle around them, and then – pop – he turned into a damn great wolf – just like that! I tell you, my heart was in my mouth, but I couldn't take my eyes off him. As you can imagine, I kept as quiet as a dead man. Please don't think I'm joking, I wouldn't lie about this for all the money in the world.

Next he began to howl horribly, a dreadful, bloodcurdling sound, and ran off at full speed into the woods. By now I was half crazed with fear. I drew my sword and staggered over shakily to look at his clothes. I couldn't believe what I was staring at – they had all turned to stone! Terrified, I made my way alone along the road, stabbing at shadows in case he came back to kill me. Trembling and weak I reached my pretty Melissa's house and nearly fainted into her arms.

Far from being sympathetic, Melissa had her own news. She's a hard woman at times:

L·V·P·V·S

"Pull yourself together," she snapped "and listen. If only you had been here sooner you might have been able to help us. A huge wolf broke in, attacked all our sheep and shed their blood like a butcher. But master wolf didn't make fools out of us, our slave stabbed him in the neck with a spear."

I spent the night at Melissa's with my sword by my side. There was no way I was going back along that road in the dark. But as you may imagine I couldn't sleep. As soon as it was daylight I hurried back to my master's house. When I passed the spot where the soldier's clothes had been, there was nothing to be seen but a ghastly pool of blood.

When I finally got home I found the soldier in bed, bleeding like an ox in the slaughterhouse. A doctor had been called and he was busy dressing a deep gash in the fellow's neck. It was then I realised he was a werewolf. After that I could not look him in the face or sit down to a meal with him. What was I supposed to say to him? "Excuse me, about the other night when you turned into a wolf..."

You don't believe my story? Well please yourself. May all your guardian spirits punish me if I'm lying.

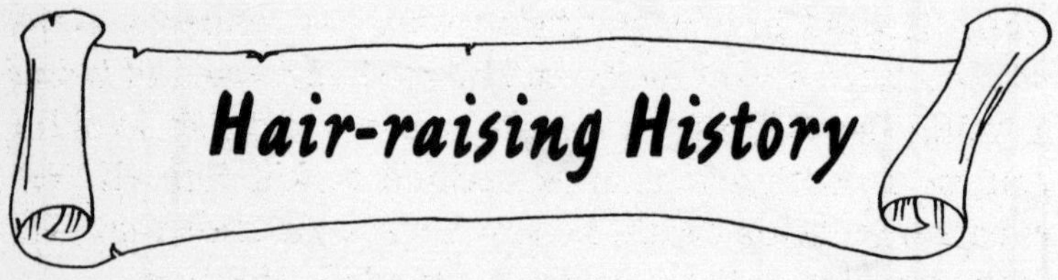

Petronius' tale is two thousand years old and includes several creepy aspects used in many werewolf horror stories and films that came later:

1. The scary switch from man to wolf occurs during a full moon.
2. The transformation happens in a graveyard.

3. The soldier has to take his clothes off, as if he is removing something that makes him uniquely human, before he changes shape. Then he pees in a circle around the clothes, like a wolf marking out his territory.
4. Once the spell has worked, the werewolf must go back to the same place to become human again.
5. The wound given to the werewolf still hurts when he turns back into a human. This is meant to prove that the story is true.

Did Petronius believe in Werewolves?

It's likely that Petronius didn't take his story seriously. The *Satyricon* was intended to be a humorous book for educated and sophisticated Roman readers. It was written to show the kind of foolish tales ex-slaves tell each other. But although Petronius wrote it for laughs, Niceros' after-dinner story is a vivid version of a popular superstition.

Stylish Suicide

What happened to Petronius? Ah yes, the messy death! Petronius ran out of luck in AD66 when jealous rivals at court accused him of plotting to kill the emperor. Nero was known for his cruelty and anyone suspected of being a traitor faced hours of torture before death. To avoid a painful execution Petronius decided to kill himself. Yet even when facing death, he was always the showman. He made sure his stylish suicide was the talk of Rome.

He had a plan to die in the same laid-back way he had lived, by enjoying himself first. Petronius ordered his slaves to cut his wrists, then when he had bled a little, he had them bind the wounds to stop the blood flow. Friends were invited round to watch and keep him company with lively conversation, stories and love poems. At intervals his veins were opened and closed again, and each time he

lost more blood and became weaker. This bizarre farewell party lasted through the night until Petronius died. Typically, his last act was to write a rude letter to Nero, telling the evil emperor exactly what he thought of him.

Where did Petronius get his Werewolf Ideas?

Petronius might have written the best ancient werewolf story but it was far from being the first. As an educated Roman he would have heard many legends of wolves, magic and shape-shifting. Prepare yourself for some of the classical shivers that may have inspired him:

Gone to the Dogs

Around 2000BC the *Epic of Gilgamesh* told of the spiteful goddess Ishtar. One of her devoted worshippers, a shepherd, made a sacrifice to Ishtar that didn't please her. In revenge she turned him into a wolf. His own wolf hounds then turned on their master, killed and ate him – as Ishtar knew they would! The poor shepherd had trained them to attack any wolves near his sheep. The dogs were just doing their job.

Don't Mess with Zeus

You probably know the story of Noah's Ark in the Bible. But did you know the Ancient Greeks had a flood myth with surprising similarities – but their version is much, much nastier.

The scene was Arcadia, a wild and mountainous area of Greece. Some Greeks said Arcadia was older than the moon and the home of witches. It was a land of limestone ridges and remote valleys surrounded by forests. The soil was thin and it was hard to scratch a living. Hard-working farmers and herdsmen kept an eye on the tree line for raids by wolf packs.

The first King of Arcadia, Lykaon, ordered his people to worship the most powerful Greek god, Zeus. To make sure

he pleased the mighty one, the King offered him a special sacrifice – a baby. But the plan backfired, Zeus was furious. He destroyed Lykaon's palace with a lightning bolt and turned him into – you've guessed it – a wolf.

Werewolf Poetry

The Roman poet Ovid, wrote a startling verse on Lykaon's transformation:

He tried helplessly to speak; from that instant
His jaws were splattered with foam, and he ached for blood.
He raged amongst the flocks and panted for slaughter.
His skin was transformed into hair, his limbs became crooked.
He was a wolf – his eyes glittered cruelly, the image of fury.

Werewolves in Deep Waters

Lykaon ran into the forest and was blessedly never seen again. Unfortunately his sons took over, and a grisly bunch they were. After a time of murder and mayhem, news of their crimes reached Zeus and he decided to investigate. He visited them disguised as a poor traveller and, like a gang of playground bullies, they saw a chance to have their usual cruel fun. They invited the traveller for a meal of 'umble' soup – gut soup that is – sheep's guts, goat's guts and the guts of the brother they had just murdered, Nyctimus!

Zeus was quivering with rage: cannibalism was disgusting to men and gods alike. He was livid that the brothers should try to trick someone into eating human flesh, especially when that someone was him. He hurled the heavy dining table aside and turned them into – wolves. All except Nyctimus who was brought back to life. However the grin on Nyctimus' face didn't last long. By now Zeus was pretty sick of humanity and decided it was

time to wipe the slate clean. He let loose a great flood, intending to destroy everyone, and leave the earth pure and fresh.

But even the best gods make mistakes. Some desperate fugitives escaped. One was Deucalion, who had been warned about the flood by his father, Prometheus, the Titan*. (If you want another truly monstrous tale look up what happened to Prometheus in a book of Greek myths.) Deucalion, the Greek Noah, built an ark, stowed plenty of supplies aboard and escaped with his wife and daughter. The ark rode the storm for nine days and finally came to rest on a mountain top. The Greeks could never agree which mountain, but Mount Parnassus was a popular choice.

If it was Parnassus, then Deucalion landed in a crowded spot. Another myth tells that as the storms began the citizens of the city of Parnassus were woken by the howling of wolves. Stumbling from their houses they saw the water rising and followed the animals up the mountain. For once the wolves weren't enemies, but saviours. Gratefully, the survivors named their new city Lycorea – *Wolf City*.

Titan: in Greek mythology the Titans were super beings, almost as powerful as the Gods.

Arcadian Werewolf Part 2

As time passed Zeus must have regretted not finishing everyone off with a few lightning bolts. Some of the Lycoreans moved to Arcadia and started the whole bad business of human sacrifice again. This time the killing went on for centuries, and if we believe the Greek geographer, Pausanias, the deaths weren't just legend – they were true.

Pausanias visited Arcadia a century after Petronius' suicide and journeyed to the heart of the barren region, Mount Lykaion. On the rugged mountain peak he witnessed the most important ritual of the year, the sacrifice to Zeus. As the sun rose in the east, the priest bowed before the ash and earth altar – and slit the throat of the offering. Turning to the crowd he held the still writhing body in his arms for all to see. And here Pausanias hesitates... he is so horror-struck that he cannot describe what he has just seen. Was it a human sacrifice???

Pausanias doesn't hold back on other details. He tells us that the Arcadians believed that every year an unfortunate worshipper at the ceremony turned into a wolf. If the shape-shifter managed to live in the wild for nine years without eating human flesh, then he or she could become human again. As you might guess, not many regained human form.

Werewolf in the Ring

Pausanias even has a sports story from Arcadia. During a sacrifice around 410BC a boxer called Damarchus tasted the guts of a boy who had been slaughtered. Immediately he turned into a wolf. Unusually, he was a well-behaved shape-shifter and didn't kill or eat anyone, so after nine years he returned to normal. The following year, however, he won an Olympic boxing contest. Can you imagine the gossip amongst the other contestants? – "Who's the hairy guy from Arcadia? Don't like the look of his teeth, do you? He used to be a werewolf, but he's not one nnnoooooooooooowwwww!"

Disappointing Dig

Was Pausanias telling the truth about Arcadia? In 1902, archaeologists excavated the site he described. They found an earth and ash altar and dug down for 1.3 metres before hitting bedrock. They certainly discovered fragments of animal bones, but there was no trace of human remains. In fact, coins and pottery indicated that the site had been used from only *c.*600BC to *c.*400BC, stopping well before Pausanias' visit. Perhaps he was simply passing on local folk tales and wasn't such a good reporter, after all.

Wolf Children – Great City

Many modern countries have adopted animals as their mascots and often claim that their people have the qualities of this national emblem – for example, the British bulldog, the Russian bear, the American eagle. In the ancient world the Romans chose the wolf. They boasted that their all-conquering city was founded with the help of a wolf. Every Roman child was taught the story of Romulus and Remus, a tale of brotherly hatred.

Romulus and Remus

Captivate your teacher with your knowledge of the classical world. Learn this famous wolf myth in ten easy steps. Begin: "Excuse me, honoured pedagogue, let me tell you a lay of Ancient Rome."

1. Numitor, the wise king of the city of Alba Longa in northern Italy, was driven from the throne by his wicked brother, Amulius. Numitor's daughter, Rhea Silvia, was forced to become a virgin priestess in the temple of Mars, god of war. Her orders from her uncle were clear, "Keep away from men or you die." Amulius

knew that if Rhea had children they might challenge him for the throne.

2. This was Amulius' big mistake. Rhea was drop-dead gorgeous, so good-looking that Mars himself fell for her. The sneaky god made love to her while she slept and, nine months later, she gave birth to twins.

3. Amulius was furious. Rhea and her children were thrown into the River Tiber. Rhea drowned but the boys were washed away by a freak current. They landed on the shore, just under the Palatine Hill, site of the future city of Rome. Their weakening cries were heard by a she-wolf – who carried the twins to her lair in a cave. She fed these strange new cubs with her own milk and curled round them at night to protect them from the cold. With each feed, wolf-strength flowed through their veins.

4. Months later the boys were discovered by a shepherd, Faustulus, who raised them as his sons. They thrived and became skilled young warriors. In a land plagued by bandits, they became expert bandit hunters.

5. The local bandit chief, Josephus was enraged. He set up an ambush and captured Remus. Josephus, however, was not the usual kill-'em-first-and-ask-questions-later kind of bandit. He had a plan. He dragged Remus before the local lord of the manor and blamed him for the crimes committed by his own gang.

6. Remus denied the accusations and, as the lord listened, he looked closely at the lad. There was something about his eyes he recognised. He interrupted the prattling bandits and demanded to know the story of Remus' life. Bet you can guess the next part? Yep, it's corny: the lord was Numitor, his grandfather.

7. Josephus and his gang were executed and both boys went happily back to their family. In a short war they helped Numitor retake his throne but that's as far as the happy ending goes. The twins decided to found their own city and chose to build by the Palatine Hill, where they had been rescued by the wolf, all those years ago. But who would rule and what was it to be called Rome or Reme?

8. They decided to let the gods pick the winner with an omen. Romulus climbed the Palatine Hill and Remus went up the nearby Aventine. Even today, these two areas of Rome are rivals. They stood patiently and waited for a sign. Suddenly the clouds parted and six great vultures swept down and circled Remus. Surely he had won! But no, the gods were only teasing. As Remus looked up he saw 12 vultures flap down to his brother.

9. Remus took his defeat badly and the brothers grew to hate one another. When Romulus marked out the city limits with a trench, in 753BC, Remus taunted him, leaping back and forth over the boundary line. "Rome will be captured as easily as this," he mocked.

10. Romulus' temper snapped and fatefully he drew his sword. The twins clashed and Remus was cut down. Rome was founded in blood and its long history was equally bloody. When the gods had sent vultures to choose between the brothers it had been a grim symbol of the future – vultures scavenge on the dead of battlefields.

Wild Wolf Festival

This cheerful tale of family rivalry inspired Romans for generations. Almost 800 years after Romulus had founded Rome, the first emperor, Augustus, used the story to boost his own power. He restored the cave in which the wolf was said to have suckled the twins and made Lupercalia, the wolf festival, into a huge celebration.

Lupercalia had been celebrated in Rome for hundreds of years. However, posh and sophisticated Romans thought it was little better than a primitive superstition – until Augustus gave it approval. Then everyone joined in.

Nightmare wolves

The wolf was feared and revered in the ancient world. Wolves were still common in Europe and most people

would have shivered in their beds as the eerie howl cut through the night. Yet, at the same time, wolf courage and cunning were qualities that humans admired. But in a world steeped in gods, magic, and shape-shifting it is not surprising that werewolves were the stuff of nightmares.

Howling with impatience for the next chapter? Read on to find the hidden horrors in the tale of Little Red Riding Hood.

Wolf Victims

Little Red Riding Hood

Fear of wolves and werewolves goes a long way back – way beyond the time of the Romans in which the last story was set. Back to the beginnings of time when people first appeared on earth and it was a struggle to find enough to eat to 'keep the wolf from the door'. There were dangers everywhere, particularly from the animals that roamed the forests. Children, especially, needed to be warned not to wander too far from their parents' side for they knew little of the hidden hazards and hungry mouths that waited to devour them.

So, as children sat round the campfire or at their mother's feet, they would be told terrifying tales. Now, at first, it doesn't seem to make a lot of sense to scare the little kiddies silly just as they're about to go to sleep. But horror stories such as Little Red Riding Hood always had a serious message – and one that children were not likely to forget.

So, are you hiding comfortably beneath the bedclothes? Have you got the light switched on? Good, then I can begin.

Who's afraid of the Big Bad Wolf?

Once upon a time, a woman gave her daughter a freshly baked loaf of bread and some milk and told her to take them to Grandma's. The little girl set off, but at the crossroads she met a werewolf.

"Where are you going, little girl?"

This should have been the moment in the story when Little Red Riding Hood high-tailed it back home, but this

was a particularly clever werewolf who looked just like you or me – well, probably more like you than me, if you don't mind! Little Red Riding Hood, her eyes wide with innocence, looked into the stranger's face and replied:

"I'm taking a loaf and a pail of milk to my grandma."

"What road are you taking," asked the werewolf, "the Needles Road or the Pins Road?"

"The Needles Road," said the little girl.

"Well, I shall take the Pins Road."

While the little girl enjoyed herself picking up needles the werewolf reached Grandma's house first.

"Are you there, Grandma?" called the werewolf in his best-possible squeaky voice.

The werewolf now showed his true nature, becoming the ravenous beast he really was. Bristles sprouted into thick matted hair and his teeth grew into needle-sharp fangs. Great globs of saliva dribbled from his hot steamy mouth as he padded slowly towards Grandma. Before the old lady could say boo to a er... wolf, he had pounced and ripped her to pieces. Werewolf did not want to spoil his appetite as much younger lunch was on its way, so he put some of Grandma's flesh in the pantry and filled a bottle with her blood for afters.

Werewolf rushed to Grandma's bed, pulled the old lady's nightcap tightly on to his head and tucked the bedspread over his long snout. He'd barely settled under the sheets when Little Red Riding Hood reached the door of the cottage and rat-a-tatted on the door.

"Just push the door open, dear, and come in," said the werewolf in his sweetest grandma voice.

"Hello, Grandma. I've brought you a hot loaf and some warm milk," said Little Red Riding Hood.

"Put them in the pantry, sweetheart," replied the werewolf. "I've left a little meat there for you and there's

a bottle of wine on the shelf – but leave some for your old gran. You'll be tired after such a long journey."

Little Red Riding Hood was soon munching her way through what was left of Grandma when the old lady's cat sidled up to her as cats do and whispered in her ear,

"A villain is she who eats the flesh and drinks the blood of her Grandmother."

The little girl gulped in horror. She'd been taught not to gulp her food but it wasn't often you snacked on Grandma – that is a real, dead Grandma. "Then... that can't be Grandma in bed," she thought as the truth slowly dawned on her. She should have known, of course: the meat was pretty tough.

"Come, my child, and cuddle in next to me," called the werewolf.

Little Red Riding Hood was too frightened to refuse. She climbed in and looked at the face under the nightcap.

"Oh, Grandma, why are you so hairy?"

"It's to keep me warm, my child."

"Oh, Grandma, why do you have such long nails?"

"It's to scratch me better, my child."

"Oh, Grandma, why do you have such big shoulders?"

"All the better to carry kindling wood, my child."

"Oh, Grandma, what are those big ears for?"

"All the better to hear you with, my child."

"Oh, Grandma, why such a big mouth?"

"All the better to eat you with, my child!"

"Grandmother, I want to go outside!"

"All right, but don't take long."

To make sure that Little Red Riding Hood did not try to run away, the werewolf tied a woollen thread to her foot before he let her go out. Once outside, the little girl tied the end of the string to a plum tree in the yard and made her escape. After a while, the werewolf became impatient and called out, but when no answer came he jumped out of the bed and saw the little girl disappearing into the distance. He chased after her but she got back home just in time. The werewolf, cheated of his prey, slunk off into the forest.

Want a Different Ending?

In this version of the story, Little Red Riding Hood escapes but poor Grandma is slain and eaten and the wolf gets away with his dastardly crime. This was too unfair for modern readers and so later versions of the story insisted that the werewolf, or wolf as he became known, got his come-uppance. In the nineteenth century the Grimm Brothers collected many folktales, including that of Little Red Riding Hood. In their version a hero woodsman comes to the rescue and kills the wolf. One, whole Grandma jumps out of the wolf's belly when it is slit open. Naturally, everyone lives happily ever after.

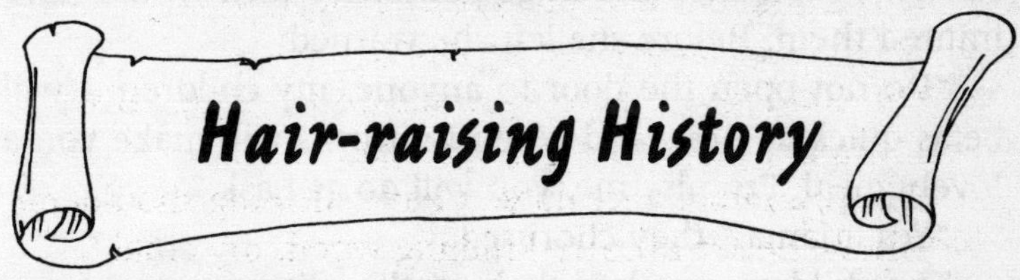

Little Red Riding Who?

Little Red Riding Hood has all the ingredients of an X-rated movie. Yet we pretend it's a nice little nursery tale. Why is it told over and over again? What dark secrets lie behind the story?

The werewolf in this story is meant to represent all the evil things that threaten us, and the tale is a terrible reminder to children of the possible consequences of talking to strangers. The earliest form of the tale can be traced back to a broad sweep of land that stretches from the Loire region of France, across the northern half of the Alps and into northern Italy. This is roughly the same area of Europe covered by the werewolf trials (see pages 52-6). As adults stopped believing in the existence of werewolves, the wolf slowly changed into a 'bogey-man'.

All over the World

Similar stories can be found in many other parts of the world, although the wolf or werewolf is often replaced with another fierce and cunning animal. There are Chinese, Japanese and Korean versions of the tale.

An Eastern Tale

Once upon a time, a widowed mother needed to go to market and sell the few vegetables she had grown in her little garden plot. She could not take her two young daughters with her, for the road to the nearby town was strewn with stones and huge potholes which would have injured them. Before she left she warned:

"Do not open the door to anyone, my children. I will be as quick as I can and when I return I will make you a lovely meal. Promise me, you will do as I ask."

"Yes, mama," they chorused.

The children watched their mother disappearing down the road carrying the baskets of vegetables suspended at either end of a pole which she carried over her shoulder. As the mother turned the bend in the road the two children pushed the door shut and slid the bolts into place.

A short time later, the mother met a tiger on the road. "Good morning, mother," said the tiger politely, "those are heavy baskets you're carrying. Are you going far?"

"Good morning, Tiger. You will forgive me if I don't stop but I need to return from market for I have left my two little daughters all alone in the house."

"Well then, dear lady. Worry no longer." And with one great pounce he pinned the mother to the ground and ate her up. Licking his lips at such a tasty start to the day he realised that there was ever such a tiny place still left in his stomach for more – to be precise; two little girls.

Tiger retraced the mother's steps and arrived at the house where the two little girls were playing in the straw, looking forward to a scrumptious meal when their mother returned. Little did they know that their mother had become the meal itself.

"Cooeee," called Tiger, "open the door, little lambs (the thought of juicy little lambs set him drooling all over his stripes). It's your great-aunt come to see her little pigeons." (The thought of two plucked and plump pigeons increased his drool to a slippery stream that formed a puddle at his feet.) The children rushed to the door and pulled the bolts back and there, there was a... tiger. Tiger tried to calm them down.

"Don't be afraid, my little ones. I met your mother on the road and she asked me to call on you to make sure you were all right. Now, let's snuggle up in bed and then I'll make a lovely meal of you... er... I mean for you."

The eldest daughter climbed into bed and cuddled Tiger.

"You seem a little peckish, my dear. Here's a little tit-bit for you." And Tiger passed a sliver of flesh to the eldest girl.

The little girl looked at what she was offered in horror for she recognised by the ring on the piece of flesh that it was, in fact, the finger of her mother.

"Oh, Great-aunt, forgive me. I must go out," for the little girl realised that she was in extreme danger and needed to escape the clutches of the Tiger.

"Well, if you must, my child," Tiger said with considerable irritation. "Here, I'll just slip this rope around you so you don't get lost."

Once in the garden the little girl attempted to hide in a tree but was discovered by Tiger when he became tired of waiting for her.

"Come down, silly child. What on earth are you doing up there?" called out Tiger to the child in the branches.

"I've trapped some birds to cook for your tea, dear Great-aunt. I won't be long. Do go inside the house and boil some water so we can cook them," replied the little girl.

The child shook the branches, to make it appear that she had caught the birds and they were fluttering to be free.

"Very well, my dear," called the Tiger through the dense screen of leaves. "Don't be long."

Several minutes later, the little girl returned to the house clutching several mysterious objects to her chest – for she had substituted stones for the imaginary birds. The water was boiling nicely on the stove and the little girl dropped the stones into the scalding water. Balancing the pan carefully so as not spill a drop, the little girl delicately carried the boiling water towards Tiger.

"Open wide, dear Great-aunt," requested the little girl as she poured the boiling water down the open throat of Tiger. The creature clutched its throat, staggered a few steps and then collapsed to the floor writhing in agony until he fell, silent and quite dead.

Myth and Magic

Werewolves have been connected to mystery and magic from the very earliest times. The idea of humans turning into animals is an extremely ancient one. Some of the earliest traces of this belief can be found in cave paintings around the world. At Trois Frères in southern France, an

image of a sorcerer dances in the flickering firelight. His ears are alert, he has a shaggy wolf-like neck and he wears a pair of antlers. His legs and feet look human but the upper part of his body has become that of an animal. We do not know the meaning of these paintings but we know that whoever painted them went to considerable trouble both in preparing the colours and carrying out the painting deep inside the darkest recesses of the caves. Those who have studied the paintings believe them to have been done for magical reasons. Dressed as an animal, these ancient hunters made homage to the spirits of the animals and begged their forgiveness for killing them.

The Wolf as Death

Wolves have always been associated closely with death. In some tribes the bodies of the dead are left out in the open to be eaten by scavenging animals – vultures and wolves. It is believed that this enables the spirit to be released to the heavens.

In Ancient Egypt, Anubis was the jackal-headed god of death and in Greek mythology, Charon, the ferryman who carried the dead across the River Styx, had wolf ears. You will have read about the influence the wolf had in Ancient Rome in chapter one. There are many stories of the savagery and power of the wolf.

Saxon Wolves

Such a feared and hated animal as the wolf was bound to come under attack. Here are some ways in which the Saxons showed their dislike.

An outcast, usually a robber, murderer or thief was known as a 'wolf-head'.

Short of money? Then you would be paid a large reward for every real wolf's head you brought in or, if there were too many to carry, then the wolf's tongue would be enough.

Saxon King Edgar hit on a neat little idea to keep one of his subjects under control and to clear the forests of wolves. In AD985 he ordered the troublesome Idwal to send him three hundred wolf skins. This not only kept Idwal out of mischief but also killed a good number of wolves in the kingdom.

War on Wolves

In the thirteenth century wolves were wiped out from England. King Edward I decided to make a sweeping change when he employed a Peter Corbet and other hunters 'to take and destroy all the wolves they can find'.

Wolves clung on a little longer in Scotland, probably until about the seventeenth century. Tradition has it that the last one was killed as late as 1848.

Ireland is well-known for its tall stories and, naturally, boasted of a 'super' wolf. This may have been a special breed that grew in size because it hunted the enormous Giant Elk. These wolves got troublesome between the 1350s and 1380s, and law after law followed to try to rid the country of the brutes. A special hound was even bred

to hunt them down – the Irish wolfhound. You may have seen one of these monsters taking its owner for a walk!

In the rest of Europe it proved far harder to get rid of wolves as they covered a vast area. In France most of the packs had disappeared by 1800 but it wasn't until 1927 that the last few were killed. Most disappeared from Scandinavia in the nineteenth century but lone individuals can still be found today deep in the forests. In southern Europe the governments were a little more relaxed and the Italian wolf, for example, lives on.

Farmers, ranchers and hunters were ruthless in their destruction of the wolf in the United States and recent attempts in 1998 to re-introduce it have been fiercely resisted. Several wolves that were introduced along the New Mexico border, for example, were found dead several months later from gunshot wounds and strangling. The hunt for the killers had all the drama of a murder inquiry. The authorities tried to hush it up and blame the deaths on a mysterious, fatal disease. The FBI were called in and rewards of $10,000 were posted. But no one squealed. The authorities got the message and called off the project. No one wanted a wolf as a neighbour!

His Great-great-great Granddaddy was a Wolf

Yes, I know your little furry canine friend would attack nothing more harmful than a slipper, but the truth of the matter is that 140,000 years ago he or she was a savage hunter and the enemy of humans. Scientists have proved by DNA* testing 67 breeds of dog and comparing with 162 wolves in Europe, America, Asia and Arabia that your faithful friend was first domesticated about 135,000 years ago from, as you might expect, the WOLF! The first dogs would have looked exactly like wolves but over the years they were bred to do particular jobs such as chasing rabbits down their burrows or rounding up sheep. Over hundreds of generations their looks gradually changed – as did their attitude to people! And what does your doggy think of all this? He probably regards one member of the family as leader of the pack and the rest of the family as fellow dogs.

DNA: these are tiny molecules that make us who we are. They have all the genetic information which makes different species of animals.

Fear of Rabies

Our old fear of wolves may also be closely connected to the terrible disease of rabies. Most wolves do not often go mad or attack people but those that do are very dangerous. Once someone displays the symptoms of the disease there is no cure unless they are inoculated quickly. Victims become terrified of water and foam at the mouth.

In areas of Russia where there are large populations of wolves, many carry the rabies virus. Records from that country show that wolves attacked two hundred and eighteen people between 1763 and 1891 of whom 34 per cent died from rabies. A more terrible recent case occurred in Russia on the morning of 8 February 1980 when ten peasants were attacked by a rabid wolf near Soleny village. The victims were taken by aeroplane to a nearby hospital where they received intensive anti-rabies treatment. All, fortunately, survived.

Is there Really a Big Bad Wolf?

Today, we still use the wolf as a symbol for cunning. A young man who chases after girls is called a 'wolf' and probably 'wolf-whistles' at them. When someone is not what they seem, we describe them as a 'wolf in sheep's clothing'.

But have wolves been treated fairly? Find out in the last chapter and make up your mind.

France, The Werewolf Files

The Jura in France is a remote area of forests and mountains. Towards the end of the 1600s the Jura became the centre of a weird werewolf scare. Belief in shape-shifting was so common that between 1570 and 1670 over five hundred people were executed for witchcraft and lycanthropy*.

The Jura, Autumn 1573

This time a little girl was missing. Fear and anger swept through towns and villages. Not again! Rumours spread like a forest fire:

"A werewolf is on the prowl. Old Meynier, the butcher, saw it with his own eyes."

"It was seen lurking around Espagny last week."

"How many children has it killed now, six or seven?"

"I'm frightened to let my girls out till it's caught."

"It attacked a group of travellers near Salvange. If they hadn't been on horseback they would have been torn apart."

"Why has nothing been done? It's a scandal."

Members of the District Court at Dôle knew they had to act quickly. The peasants were jittery, already terrified

Lycanthropy: has two meanings: 1. A person magically turning into a wolf or 2. A person who believes he or she has turned into a wolf.

by news of civil war and angry about the high taxes they were forced to pay. A werewolf scare could spark riots or even a rebellion. After a brief debate they gave the people new powers to protect themselves:

> ***Dôle, Thirteenth day of September, 1573***
> ***To prevent any danger the Court does permit citizens to gather with pikes, javelins, guns, clubs and sticks to chase and to pursue the werewolf in every place were they may find or seize him; to tie or to kill him, without fear of punishment.***

The law was well-meant, but it let loose an unruly and dangerous armed mob. It was chance for those with black minds to settle old scores.

Two months later, near Authune, a little girl was savaged by a wolf as she played in a meadow. Villagers working nearby heard her cries and the baying of a wolf. Knowing a werewolf was on the loose, they rushed to the rescue. The peasants reported later that the wolf was huge, far bigger than a normal animal. And as they dodged its snapping jaws some of them recognised human features, the face of a neighbour, Gilles Garnier.

Screaming, shouting and beating the wolf with their tools, they chased the beast away. The girl was saved, but she was barely alive and bleeding from five ferocious bites. As they carried her home they anxiously talked over what they had witnessed. They were frightened and the finger of suspicion was pointed at a helpless old man.

Victim

Poor Garnier was a natural victim. He was odd and this made him the subject of gossip and distrust. Locals knew Garnier was an outsider, originally from Lyon. Since he was rarely seen, his nickname was 'the hermit of St

Bonnet'. He lived miles from anywhere, with his wife Apolline. The pair were desperately poor, their home a crude hut with a turf roof and walls covered in lichen. They rarely talked to others.

Garnier had led a hard life and it showed. He was a gloomy looking man with a pale, drawn face and grey complexion, discoloured as if he had been bruised in a fight. His deep-set eyes were hidden by big, bushy eyebrows, which met across his forehead. Even the way he stood marked him out. Garnier had a stooped back and walked with a stumble, as if he couldn't stand upright. Once seen, his looks were not forgotten.

Arrest

"Garnier's a strange one," said the tattle-mongers. "What's he doing hiding out there in the woods with his wife?"

"Mark my words," grumbled the busybodies. "Those bushy eyebrows are the sign of a werewolf. Everyone knows it."

"What about that stoop of his?"' agreed the trouble-makers. "He's spent so long running on all fours, like a wolf, he can't stand up properly anymore."

A few days later another child, a boy of ten went missing, and Gilles Garnier and Apolline were arrested. He was tortured and confessed to a string of murders. Agreeing to anything to stop the pain, the details he gave were gruesome. Yes, using a magic ointment given to him by the devil, he could shape-shift. It was he who had attacked the injured girl while he was a wolf. The peasants had not been mistaken. The boy, too, was his prey, strangled with his hairy paws. When his hunger had got the better of him, he had torn off one of the poor lad's legs with his fangs and eaten the tender thigh. And then there were the other killings.

Confession and Execution

Garnier admitted that in August he had slaughtered a twelve-year-old boy in a pear orchard, near the village of Perrouze. "Despite of the fact that it was Friday" (a day on which good Christians did not eat meat) he had been about to devour the boy when he was disturbed and scampered off. Early in October, his evil work had not been interrupted and he had savaged a ten-year-old girl in a vineyard, near La Serre. He tore at her with his teeth and claws and so enjoyed the taste of her 'sweet flesh' that he took a limb back for his wife.

The judge at Garnier's trial, Henri Camus, made sure there were no doubts about his conviction. He drummed up over 50 people willing 'to bear witness' against the hermit. Amongst them were the most educated citizens of the community. One of them was Daniel d'Ange, who wrote:

> *'Gilles Garnier had no way of looking after his family. As sometimes happens with simple and desperate folk, he took to wandering into the woods and wild places. In this state he was met by a devil in the form of a man. The devil told him he would teach him to change at will into a wolf, lion or leopard. Since the wolf is better known in this country than the other wild beasts, Garnier chose to disguise himself in that shape. The devil gave him an ointment with which he rubbed himself when he wanted to shape-shift.'*

There was never any doubt of the verdict. Garnier was found guilty and condemned to death by burning. It was the custom in France that a criminal who pleaded guilty would be shown a little mercy. Burning was a fearsome death, so he or she would be strangled first to spare them the agony. But Camus knew the mood of the district was explosive. Garnier was to be treated harshly to show that

the law in the Jura was strong. Camus pronounced his sentence.

> *'Seeing that Gilles Garnier has, by the evidence of reliable witnesses and his own confession been proven guilty of witchcraft and shape-shifting, this Court condemns the said Gilles, to be this day taken in a cart to the place of execution, accompanied by the executioner. He shall be tied to a stake and burned alive.*

Garnier died on 18 January 1574. Yet the fear of sorcery was so great that his ashes were raked together and scattered to the four winds. Only when Garnier was dust in the air could the people of Dôle sleep easily; now even the most powerful spells couldn't bring him back.

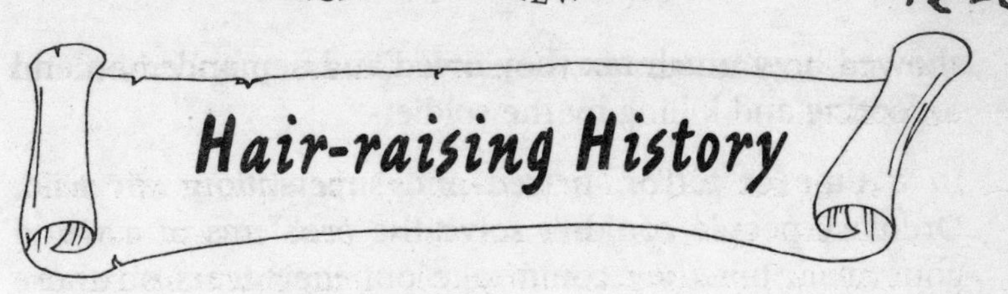

A Time for Hysteria

Werewolf fever was a symptom of a dangerous time in French history. It seemed that God had turned his face from France and the Devil stalked the land.

Famine: At the end of the sixteenth century there was year after year of cold, wet weather. Crops rotted in the fields and people starved. With hunger came disease, and plague-carts collected the dead in towns and cities.

War: Years of bloody civil war tore the country apart as Catholics fought Protestants.

On the 24 August 1572 thousands of Protestants* in Paris were slaughtered during the St Bartholomew's Day massacre. By the 1590s the tide of war had turned and a Protestant army surrounded Paris. The Catholics* trapped inside the city walls were so hungry that they ate anything – grass, dogs, cats, rats and birds. Bread was made with flour ground from the bones of dead animals and humans.

Taxes: War costs money and led to high taxes. Across southern France peasants rioted, sometimes joined by workers from the towns. They burned the records which

Protestants: Christians who broke away from the Catholic Church and do not accept the leadership of the Pope.
Catholics: Christians who believe the Pope in Rome is God's spokesman on Earth.

showed how much tax they owed and demanded an end to looting and killing by the soldiers.

In a time of terror, hatred and superstition ran wild. Ordinary people couldn't solve the problems of a world gone mad, but they could take out their fears on those suspected of being werewolves.

Judge Dread

What do you expect from a judge? Fairness? Justice? Then be glad you never appeared before Henri Boguet, Supreme Judge of the St Claude district of Burgundy. His hands were stained with the blood of the innocent and the insane. Boguet wrote *Discours des Sorciers* (*Knowledge of Sorcerers*), a best-seller which was published twelve times between 1598 and 1616. The book became a guide for witch- and werewolf-hunters across Europe – a guide to torture and terror.

Discours includes the pitiful stories of the judge's victims and the evidence he looked for to catch them. Spare a tear for one, Clauda Gaillard:

Clauda was condemned by a neighbour, Jeanne Perrin. The two women were walking in the woods when Clauda disappeared behind a bush. An instant later a tail-less wolf loomed out of the undergrowth. Jeanne was horror-struck, she was sure the wolf had hind legs, like those of a human. Shrieking in terror she made the sign of the cross and ran for her life.

Later Jeanne warily confronted Clauda. What had she made of the strange wolf? Hadn't she been terrified? Yet far from being excited Clauda calmly replied " If I'd seen the wolf I wouldn't have been worried. It wouldn't have hurt me." What could be more suspicious than this? Jeanne reported Clauda to Boguet.

But Jeanne's accusation was just the start. At Clauda's trial Boguet heard other neighbours, and even relatives, add their charges: she had caused the death of six goats belonging to Peter Perrier; she had cured a sick mare, but only after she had made it ill first; she had danced with witches and praised the Devil; she had turned into a wolf.

From the moment he began to question Clauda, Boguet was sure of her guilt. In his mind the proof was clear. He wrote, 'No one ever saw her shed a single tear… sorcerers do not cry because they cannot change their sinful lives, and as we all know, tears are the first sign of repentance'.

A Sham Trial

Look at the details again. The flimsy evidence convinced Boguet, but what do you think?

Panic: Jeanne Perrin ***thought*** she saw a strange wolf, and frightened herself so badly she could have seen anything!

Common-sense: Clauda said the wolf ***would not harm her***, but she was quite right, wolves only attack people if they are desperate. Usually they keep well away from them.

Superstition: The accusations of the other neighbours were ***superstitious nonsense***, probably based on jealousy or fear. Between 1550 and 1650 over 90 per cent of those charged with witchcraft or shape-shifting were women, usually old and helpless. In most cases they were accused by neighbours who had suffered misfortunes such as an illness or the death of child or animal.

Witnesses: Even Bouget admitted that there was ***never more than one witness*** to any of the crimes that Clauda was accused of. So much for supporting evidence!

Fear: As for the fact that Clauda didn't cry, ***she was probably so frightened that her tear ducts had dried up***. Bouget took this as the mark of the devil because he had read this in another book about hunting witches, *The Evil of Sorcerers* by Jean Bodin.

Poor Clauda, she was doomed from the start of her trial and died at the stake.

The Torture Chamber

Most of the people burned as werewolves in France, including Gilles Garnier and Clauda Gaillard, admitted their own guilt. They knew this would lead to an

agonising death, so why didn't they deny the charges to the bitter end? The answer is brutal – torture. Since the courts believed suspects were in league with the devil, pain was used to force them to tell the truth and shame the Devil. The tools for torture were awesomely cruel.

Tools of Terror

The Wrack: a pulley that stretched the body, tore sinews and pulled bones out their sockets.

Thumbscrews: a small vice that crushed thumbs and fingers.

Spanish Boots: a larger version of thumbscrews, for crushing feet.

Strappado: prisoners were hoisted into the air by their hands – but cruelly their arms were first tied behind their backs. As they were lifted off the ground their own weight dislocated their shoulders.

Hot Irons: red hot pokers and pincers that burned and ripped flesh.

Boiling Resin: used to test if someone was a werewolf or not. The prisoner's fingers were dipped into the resin: if they were unharmed they were innocent. Fat chance!

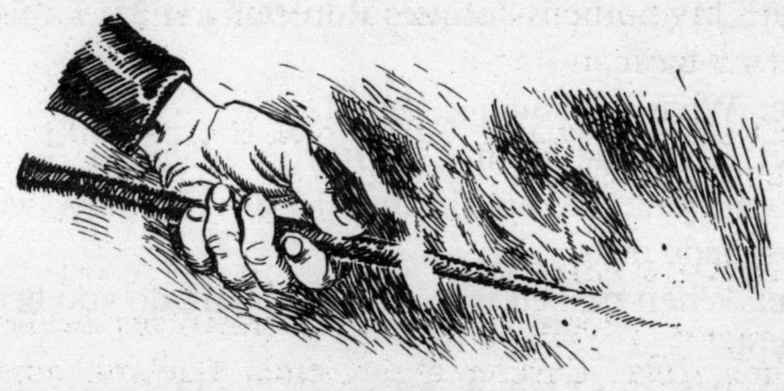

Often, a tour of the torture chamber was all that was needed to make a prisoner confess. A glance at the glowing irons... a few moments strapped to the wrack... feeling the weight of the thumbscrews... almost guaranteed terror.

What would you have done? Bravely defied the guards, yelling "Do your worst."? Probably not. Like most people you would have begged, "All right, just tell me what to say." The truth didn't matter, once someone was a suspect, like Clauda they were nearly always proven guilty. If they bravely denied the charges against them, even under torture, the court inquisitors knew why. They were the servants of the devil and the forces of evil were helping them stand the pain. The answer? More pain.

The Confession

Even after threats or torture some prisoners couldn't be relied on to confess properly. They were read a list of prepared questions and only allowed to give simple answers. Read this confession carefully. It was made by Jacques Roulet in 1598, a beggar found near the body of a fifteen-year-old boy. Jacques was dressed in rags and had shreds of flesh stuck under his fingernails.

Judge: What is your name and your work?

Roulet: My name is Jacques Roulet, I am 35; I am poor and a beggar.

Judge: What are you accused of?

Roulet: Of being a thief; of having offended God. My parents gave me an ointment; I do not know what it was made of.

Judge: When rubbed with this ointment, do you become a wolf?

Roulet: No. But I killed and ate the child. I was a wolf.

Judge: Were you dressed as a wolf?

Roulet: I was dressed as I am now. My hands and face were bloody because I had been eating the flesh of the child.

Judge: Do your hands and feet turn into the paws of a wolf?

Roulet: Yes, they do.

Judge: Does your head become like that of a wolf – your mouth bigger?

Roulet: I do not know how my head was at the time; I used my teeth. My head was as it is today. I have wounded and eaten many other little children. I have worshipped with witches.

Jacques was probably guilty of cannibalism. His crime was disgusting but did that make him a werewolf? Are you convinced, or is Jacques being led by the judge? He is certainly confused and unsure whether, and when, he shape-shifted or not.

Unfortunately Jacques was caught in a vicious circle of fear. The more people confessed, the more the authorities believed there was a werewolf epidemic. The more the authorities believed there was an epidemic, the more they used torture to trap suspects, and the more they used torture the more people confessed. And so on and on... But fate took an unexpected turn for Jacques...

The Tide Turns

Jacques Roulet was sentenced to death in August 1598, but was allowed to appeal to the Parliament of Paris. Astonishingly his sentence was changed. It was decided that Roulet was mad and that he should be sent to the mental hospital of St Germain-des-Pres for two years. During this time he was to be taught religion and the

mercy of god, 'which he had forgotten in his utter poverty'. It was an act of kindness rare in such a frenzied time, but marked the beginning of a change of heart by the authorities.

Doctors began to question whether shape-shifting was a fact or a delusion, and if far too many victims were mad rather than evil. They explained lycanthropy in a new way, as an hallucination. The shape-shifting was only happening in the minds of the insane and this drove them to act like wolves, even to the point of attacking others ferociously. Gradually the courts began to listen. Even so it took another thirty years before werewolf fever ended in France.

The Wild Beast of Gévaudan

Real wolves rarely threaten people, except when they are desperate. Yet sometimes rogue leaders lead their packs on raids against flocks, farms and even villages and towns. In the 1760s a giant red wolf, the Beast of Gévaudan, struck terror across six districts of southern France. Rumours ran wild and soon the country was gripped by another werewolf scare.

The Languedoc Region 1764–7

The Beast was back. It slipped quietly through the town of Mazel-de-Grèzes, following a familiar scent – the scent of the fourteen-year-old boy it had killed yesterday. Nose twitching, it stalked towards his home. Locked inside, in their private grief, his family were making the funeral arrangements. Standing on hind legs, almost like a man, the Beast peered in, tongue lolling between stained teeth.

The boy's father brushed his tears aside, a sudden chill spinning down his spine. He glanced at the window and jumped up in shock. Yellow eyes stared back into his own. His thoughts reeled: *The Beast here! In daylight! In the village! What devil is this?*

Screaming in anger he snatched up his axe and ran for the door. Yet by the time he had flung it open and dashed to the window the apparition was gone. He slammed the axe blade into the ground, crying in frustration. Yet he should not have been ashamed that the Beast had escaped his anger. The incident at Mazel was one more killing, one more vain sighting, in a long-running hunt.

The Beast began its reign of terror in the district of Gévaudan, high in the mountainous Massif Central. The first kill was discovered in June 1764 near the little town of Langogne. Within five months, eleven people had died, all but two of them women and children. One unfortunate woman was slaughtered in her own garden, in the hamlet of Estrets. There was no doubt about the fate of the victims, since the beast had left its grisly trademark. Their faces had been torn away.

Frequent sightings soon added to the terror of the local peasants. Stunned eyewitnesses claimed the Beast was huge, over two metres long, with teeth like small knives. Some said it could kill with a single blow of its mighty tail, others that it could leap enormous heights and run with supernatural speed. Most agreed its fur was not wolf grey, but red, like burnished copper. Although few caught more than a glimpse of the Beast, more smelt it. It left a fiendish stink in its evil wake.

It was soon clear that the Beast was no ordinary, slinking wolf. But if not, what was it? Speculation flowed thick and fast:

It was a hyena escaped from a nearby fair at Beaucaire.

No, it was a large monkey, like a gorilla. It had been seen fording a deep river, walking upright like a human.

Nonsense, it was so deadly it had to be the offspring of a wolf and a bear, come over the Alps from Italy.

Yes, it was a crossbreed, but from two fairground animals, a hyena and a tiger.

The peasants listened to the rumours and snorted. They knew in their bones what the beast was – a werewolf. They agreed that if you listened to the evidence carefully there was proof enough. A young boy had been attacked by the Beast and had had a miraculous escape. He had bravely wrestled with it before it fled, perhaps

shocked that he had fought back. In the struggle the boy had glanced at its belly and seen a row of buttons on the skin. Would a child lie about a detail like this? It was obvious that the Beast was a werewolf, why else would it wear a waistcoat? And then there was that woman going to Mass. A hairy man had walked by her side for some distance before he suddenly vanished. Like a demon! Surely the authorities could see that there was a sorcerer at work.

The local nobleman, M. de Labarthe wrote mockingly to a friend:

> *'You would laugh to hear all they say about it: it takes tobacco, talks, becomes invisible, boasts in the evening about its exploits of the day, worships the devil, does penance for its sins. Every man and woman has his own story about it.'*

But it was easy to laugh when you were safe behind the walls of a château.

As the death toll mounted, the army was called in. A patrol of dragoons (cavalry with firearms), led by Captain Jean Duhamel, combed the forest for months. They caught glimpses of shapes, they charged after shadows, they opened fire at quivering bushes but they did not catch the elusive Beast. Even a reward of a thousand crowns, a fortune, failed to spur the hunters to the kill.

When men failed, the Catholic Church tried. As 1764 drew to a close, the Bishop of Mende sent out his Christmas letter. The beast was a punishment from God for the sins of the people, he wrote. If they prayed hard and begged forgiveness then this curse would be taken from them. But the slaughter went on during 1765 and the number of dead was soon over fifty.

It was not until September that the Beast was cornered. Day after day hundreds of men tramped through the forest of la Tenaziere, armed with pitchforks, axes and guns. On September 20 the Beast made a break and ran into the gun sights of a professional hunter, Monsieur Beauterme. Coolly taking aim as the monster dashed towards him, Beauterme fired and watched with satisfaction as his target collapsed, convulsed and died. He was lucky, the Beast had been struck down only a few metres from the smoking barrel of his rifle.

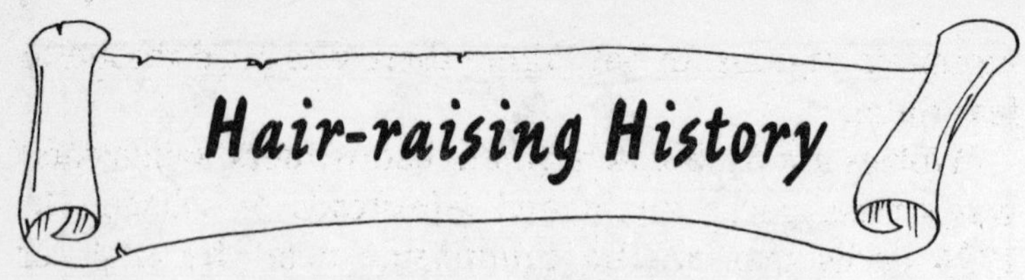

What was the Wild Beast of Gévaudan?

The king had been anxiously following events and the body was sent for him to inspect at the Palace of Verşailles. It measured 1.72 metres from nose to tail tip and stood 81 centimetres high. A court surgeon dissected the beast and reported that he thought it was more likely to be a hyena than a wolf. However, he had little experience of animals on which to base his opinions.

Historians disagree about what really happened, but it seems unlikely that there was only one Beast. Sightings and slayings had taken place many kilometres apart on the same day. This was too large a territory, even for a super-beast. There were still plenty of wolves in the Languedoc area and the probable explanation is that the killings were the work of a pack, or even several packs, of wolves. The lone hyena may have been responsible for a few of the attacks. Separate killings became linked as panic spread through the region and the legend of the Beast was born.

Real Wolf Danger

France is a large country and even today there are areas of wilderness where animals, such as wild boar, can roam undisturbed by humans. Two hundred years ago this was even more true and wolves thrived in forest and

mountain regions. In hard times there was good reason to fear them.

Wolves are flesh-eaters and in bad winters, when food was scarce, packs threatened farmsteads or villages. In 1796 packs overran the countryside near the cities of Orléans and Chartres. Over five thousand wolves were killed in 1797, and in the early 1800s the problem wasso great that the authorities organised wolf hunts to keep their numbers down.

Eighty years later the fear lingered on. In the winter of 1890 young Léon Ganachaud saw wolves sneak out of the forests to scavenge near his home, in the commune of Ambérac. Looking back as an old man, the memories were still painful; two wolves killed his dog and ran off with the body. After this Léon was not allowed out at night, and his thirteen-year-old sister, who minded the sheep, was warned to keep away from the woods.

Werewolves, the Graveyard Link

Although wolves can be good hunters, working as a pack to bring down their prey, life is easier for them if they can scavenge. Something already dead and rotting would be a prime morsel. From a wolf point of view, what better place for a good juicy meal than a graveyard? From a human point of view, what could be more terrible, devilish and shocking?

Graveyards in the past were not always the neat and orderly places we think of now. Only the very rich could afford a wooden coffin and a deep grave. Most people were buried in simple cloth shrouds, perhaps only a metre below ground. In times of famine or a plague the glut of dead meant hasty graves, dug with even less care.

Such poor cemeteries were easily disturbed: a corpse rotten and bloated with gases might loosen the earth above; poor drainage could waterlog a grave, pushing the body upwards while a shallow burial often left part of the body exposed once the ground had settled. Was it any wonder then that wolves came to graveyards to scavenge and that outraged peasants, seeing their flitting shapes in the dark, believed they were werewolves? Reports were so frequent in France that werewolf hunters gave a special name for the kind of monster that preferred dead flesh to fresh kills – the *loublin*.

The Vampire Link

In eastern Europe reports of wolves raiding graves sparked another legend – double trouble, the vampire-werewolf. The tale was terrifying. Locked in its coffin a corpse stirs. Knarled hands tear open the shroud and scrabble against the wooden lid. Bestial growls echo through the earth, rising into howls of pain. With demonic strength the corpse smashes open the coffin and claws its way to the surface. From the blackened soil emerges a werewolf back from the dead and in search of blood.

Gypsies however had a different story. In their folklore the wolf was the enemy of the vampire. Led by the great white wolf, packs patrolled graveyards to keep the undead in their graves. If a vampire was caught in the open it would be torn to pieces.

Werewolf Lunacy

The link between werewolves and the full moon may be aeons old. Some anthropologists* suggest that the werewolf legend may stretch back to prehistoric times when the full moon marked the beginning of the hunt.

Much of the time, prehistoric people lived by gathering food such as nuts, berries and grubs. As this was a basic diet, lacking in protein, they also needed meat. Once a month the bright light of the full moon gave hunters a chance to catch their prey at night. Since the hunt was vital for the survival of the tribe, it became an important ritual. Before they started, the men worked themselves up into a killing frenzy, becoming as ferocious as wild animals – almost like the savage change from human to werewolf. Even now the phrase 'a hunters' moon' is sometimes used to describe a full moon.

There is also some evidence that the moon alters the way people behave. It orbits the earth every 29½ days and changes the geomagnetic field* of the planet. Biologists know that this affects plants and animals, including fiddler crabs which change colour according to the lunar cycle.

Since ancient times, doctors have noticed violent changes in people during a full moon. Indeed the word 'lunacy', meaning madness, comes from the Latin for 'moon', *luna*. Until 1808, Bedlam, the London hospital for the insane, used to beat patients to stop their weird

Anthropologists: scientists who study societies and their customs.

Geomagnetic field: magnetic waves around the Earth, like a giant but very weak magnet.

behaviour as the moon waxed. Today, police officers, firemen and paramedics expect their busiest times when the moon is full. A New York ambulance driver told psychologist Arnold Lieber, "On those nights there is a holy mess of violent crimes and accidents."

Werewolf Test

Does your PE teacher grunt and growl when the moon is full? Are the backs of his hands hairy? Do his eyebrows meet in the middle? Suspicious??? Try this medieval werewolf test:

Take a piece of pure iron or steel. Be traditional, try a horseshoe. OK be boring, a stainless steel paperclip will do. Throw the metal at the suspect and prepare for a shock. If he is a real werewolf his skin will start to split at the forehead. Wait a while and he'll step naked out of his hairy suit.

However, think carefully before using this test. Just suppose you discovered your PE teacher really was a werewolf. What would you say to the Head?

"Excuse me, Miss. Can I have a word with you in confidence? It's about Mr... You see I and the rest of the class had this funny feeling about him and...(Well, go on...)"

Top Ten Tips for Werewolf Watching

If you think it's a bit rude to throw metal objects about, then keep your eyes peeled for these sure-fire signs of werewolves in human form:

1. Werewolves are often restless and anxious before they change into animal shape. They prowl about the room as if they are in cage. If a suspect is walking on all-fours, get out fast.
2. Werewolves know they are dangerous and try to get friends and family away from them before they

shape-shift. They have human emotions until the last moment but once they change they are ruthless killers. If a hairy friend begs you to leave – listen and obey!

3 In the hours before they change, werewolves gain some of the powers of the wolf – acute hearing, animal strength and an excellent sense of smell.

4 Become a fingernail spotter; werewolves have reddish, curved almond-shaped nails. Some have a long, thick nail on their left thumb – as hard as the claw of a wolf.

5 Look at the rest of the hand too. Is it very broad and hairy? If the third finger is unusually long – be cautious.

6 A not-very-helpful Russian tip – look under the tongue of a suspect to see if it has bristles. This only works if you are brave enough to ask him/her to open their mouth while you peer in. Perhaps not!

7 Being a werewolf is exhausting so shape-shifters are often pale, with sunken cheeks, black hollow eyes and swollen lips.

8 After a night drinking thick, salty blood werewolves are always very thirsty.

9 Look at the way a suspect walks. Werewolves have long swinging strides, like a prowling wolf.

10 Watch the sleeping habits of a suspect. Sleeping outside on a Wednesday or Friday when there is a full moon may trigger a change of shape. Be wary about your camping companions.

What to do when a Werewolf is on the Loose

In Hollywood films the only way to deal with a werewolf is to shoot it with a silver bullet. Folklore and legend suggest a few other possibilities:

If you are attacked look the shape-shifter in the eye and yell, "Take off your skin!" The werewolf must accept this challenge and peel off his/her hairy pelt. Then you fight, human against human. But there is a drawback to this anti-werewolf martial art; if you lose then you must put on the skin and become the werewolf yourself.

If you recognise a werewolf, yell out his/her real name and he/she must change back into a human. But how on earth are you going to recognise someone under all that hair? A good question. Look at the eyes; werewolf eyes keep their human shape and colour.

If you can catch a werewolf before he/she shape-shifts you can stop them rampaging. Lock the suspect in an escape-proof room. This must have strong walls, a reinforced door and bars at the windows. A cellar would be ideal. Don't listen to anything a changeling tells you. They will promise anything to be let free. Don't open the door until they have been quiet for at least 12 hours.

In the days of muskets*, a musket ball made from the pith of the elder tree, was said to be as good as a silver ball – and a lot cheaper.

Musket: an early type of gun, using gunpowder and lead balls rather than bullets.

King Werewolf

England does not have many werewolf stories and legends compared to France, but one is spectacular. Tricky King John, brother of Richard the Lion Heart, was a suspected shape-shifter. After his burial in Worcester Cathedral the monks heard fearful noises coming from his tomb in front of the High Altar. They dug up his corpse and 'flung the vile carcass' out of the church and on to unconsecrated ground. The king's blackened features lay there, his face twisted with a hideous grin.

Wolf Talk

The cunning and ferocity of the wolf has led to some colourful additions to the English language. Try these out in your school work.

Wolf phrases:

You've got *a wolf by the ears*... oops you're in trouble

You have *a wolf in the stomach*... you're famished

Someone is *a wolf in sheep's clothing*... they seem pleasant but watch out!

When the wolf is at the door, love flies out the window... being poor makes life hard. On your pocket money, you know this.

A friend is *crying wolf*... they pretend something is wrong so often that when they finally tell the truth you don't believe them.

Wolf words:

to wolf: to gulp food down... be greedy... hard up...

a wolf: a good bargainer... a ladies man... violent person

wolf's head: an outlaw, like Robin Hood

wolf pack: submarines attacking merchant ships

wolf cub: a cub scout

wolf-hole: a trap

wolfkin: a small wolf (an affectionate term for your little brother?)

The Kindness of Wolves

Fear of wolves has fired countless horror stories, yet there is another side to their nature which makes them good parents capable of acts of kindness to other species. Wolf parents raise their pups with great care. Members of the pack help out with feeding the females whilst they are pregnant and when the offspring are still little. The mother must stay with her young after they are born, for they cannot control their own body heat and need the protection of her warm coat to keep then warm. The young are loved and cared for by everyone. It is probably this instinct which has given rise to a number of stories where wolves have cared for abandoned human children. What follows are strange but true stories of wolf-children.

The Wolf-boy of Aveyron

The forests of Aveyron are still an isolated area of France. Two hundred years ago the dense woodlands stretched over an even greater area of countryside. In places the thickets are dense and difficult to penetrate and only a few shards of sunlight filter in to the dark recesses of the forest.

In 1797 a group of charcoal burners had moved their camp to a new site, in search of supplies of the saplings they needed to make charcoal for the iron smelting industry. This type of work was always hard and exhausting. The workers would be a long way from home, often for weeks at a time – but for some, the freedom of their way of life in the fresh open air made up for the loneliness and isolation.

As dusk settled around them, the band would draw closer to the fire, ladling rabbit stew on to plates and using their bread as a spoon to scoop the meal into their mouths. One night, two of the band heard a rustle in the undergrowth and saw a flash of white streak against the evening gloom. Breaking clear of a small bush several feet from their campfire, a naked animal scurried for the bushes on the other side of the small clearing.

"What the...?"' The taller of the two men jumped to his feet, sending the stew spluttering onto the fire. "Did you see...?" He could not finish his sentences as he tried to take in what he had just seen.

"Yes... Yes. It were a human lad – or some devilish creature like a human or werewolf." His friend completed and confirmed the taller man's wild thoughts.

Taking two firebrands, they searched the area around the camp, the firelight sending shadows dancing wildly in the evening gloom. But they could find no trace of the creature that night.

Over the next few weeks the strange animal returned, perhaps attracted by the firelight, perhaps by the sound of human voices. But the men saw little more than a streak of flesh or the glitter from its eye as it darted for cover. It appeared to be a boy but under the coat of dirt and thick matted hair they could not be sure, for he more closely resembled a wolf as he darted along on all fours.

Capture

Stories of the wolf-boy quickly spread throughout the district and at each telling they became wilder. Some versions had him disappearing in clouds of smoke, others said that he could fly between the branches of the trees, and that he mysteriously changed his shape so that he blended with the forest. There were even some who felt brave enough to hunt for him; their curiosity overcoming their fear. When the tale of this curiosity reached the ears of two unpleasant rogues who had a travelling show in which they exhibited 'freaks of nature', they were delighted at the thought of a new exhibit. Any misformed animal or deformed person could find themselves on show 'for the edification and instruction of the common man' as their posters declared. Lambs born with two

heads and bearded ladies were all 'valuable' educational tools to this pair of rogues. Or, if some monstrosity was not available then the careful use of paint and clay could help it appear to be true.

It therefore excited them to learn, when they brought their travelling show to Aveyron, that a new and 'wonderful' exhibit was available out there in the forest. Going to the charcoal burners who had first spotted the wolf-boy, they struck a deal. If they were to trap and bring the creature to them they would be handsomely rewarded.

An 'Educational' Exhibit

It took the charcoal burners three days to track down the wolf-boy and snare him in a pit covered with light branches by tempting the creature with a bait made from pieces of potato. Trussed-up on a pole they carried him out of the forest and into the hands of the fairground vendors. The creature was terrified. Taken from its natural habitat, the poor wolf-boy struggled to understand why so many people crowded around him. He puzzled at the strangely shaped trees which sprouted smoke.

All the wolf-boy knew was that he should not be here. Should not be gawked at by those beery faces nor laughed at by the hordes of human cubs who came to stare and poke sticks into his side through the bars of the cage. He watched and waited for a chance to escape. He had been taught well by his mother wolf to be cunning in the hunt.

In the evening, when he was fed, he noticed that his gaoler seemed a little unsteady on his feet. It must be that red liquid, he thought, that they seemed very fond of, for they were steadier on their feet during the day.

One evening, he pretended to be asleep in the straw when it was time to be fed. As the door of his cage whined

open and the man pushed the bowl of food towards him he threw himself against the half-open door, knocking his gaoler to the ground. Within minutes he had darted past the startled townspeople on all fours and was back in his wooded sanctuary.

Acts of Kindness

Wolf-boy remained very wary of the human kind. They had not treated him as well as the wolves of the forest. But the men would not leave him alone. Throughout the summer months, search parties crashed through the forest or lone hunters stalked their strange prey. In 1799 he was captured again. This time, the people of Averyon's curiosity had turned to pity for the poor wolf-boy and they wished him to be looked after properly. A widow on the edge of town agreed to take him in. She had no family and looked upon the foundling as if he were her own son.

After several days of kind treatment the wolf-boy began to calm down and nuzzle into the widow's side for comfort. But try as she might she could not get him to eat human food. Indeed he would eat very little apart from acorns, chestnuts, potatoes and walnuts and would refuse meat whether it was cooked or raw.

Despite the old lady's kindness, the forest seemed to call him on every breeze that wafted his face. He laughed when the wind blew through the leaves of the tree and he loved to run through the undergrowth and feel the waving grasses caress his legs. He began to stay away from the widow's care for longer spells until one day he did not return at all. He preferred to live a life of solitude in the remote mountains. Even then, local farmers felt sorry for him and, occasionally left potatoes out on the forest track for him. He was, they felt, an innocent creature of nature. During the day he could be seen swimming in the local

streams or running at great speed on all fours and laughing when the wind buffeted his face.

As the summer passed, wolf-boy began to struggle to survive. The winter of 1800 was a particularly bitter one. He could find little to eat and local people were afraid he would die from the extreme cold. A more permanent solution, they believed, was needed. In January of that year he was captured and taken to an orphanage. He was, by now, somewhere between twelve and fifteen years of age and could not speak at all, barking and howling to show his feelings. But with care and patience he was taught a few words and his speech began to be recognisable. The orphanage attendants, however, failed miserably when they tried to dress him for he would tear the clothes off his body in a fury.

Wolf-boy caused considerable scientific interest at the time. Scientists were interested in how human beings developed and wanted to know more. They wondered whether the way humans were brought up was more important than the intelligence with which they were born. Wolf-boy seemed to offer a good opportunity to study someone who, as far as they knew, had not been brought up by human beings.

Grants of money were made by the authorities to provide the wolf-boy with teachers but they had little real success and gradually the money was stopped. Much of the interest in wolf-boy faded away but he lived on and grew to manhood. The lessons he had been taught were quickly forgotten as the wild, untamed side of his nature appeared to be stronger. In 1828 wolf-man, as he had now become, passed away, having scarcely changed from the wild state in which he had been discovered.

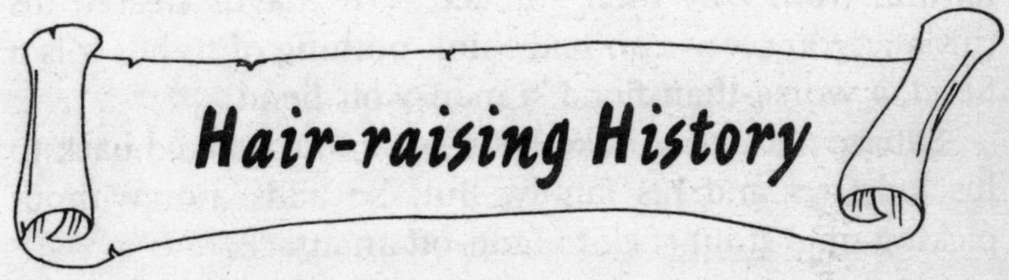

A Fear of Wolves

As you will have read in the last chapter France was besotted with fear of werewolves during the Middle Ages. These beliefs were still taken seriously well into the eighteenth and the nineteenth centuries. Sabine Baring-Gould, who collected folk tales of these wolf-fiends and published them in *The Book of Werewolves,* became interested in the subject as a result of a first-hand experience in a remote part of the French countryside.

Having found himself out late at night after visiting some ancient standing stones he made his way to a small village to hire a horse. None were available. "Then I must walk!" declared Sabine. The mayor was quick to reply. "Sir can never go back tonight across the flats, because of the – the –" and his voice dropped, "the loups-garous, the werewolves."

Wolves could still be found in the remote regions of Europe but the villagers had a very different sort of wolf in mind and one they were convinced existed. A peasant explained. "Picou tells me that he saw the werewolf only this past day's night. He was down by the hedge of his buckwheat field, and the sun had set, and he was thinking of coming home, when he heard a rustle on the far side of the hedge. He looked over, and there stood the wolf as big as a calf against the horizon, its tongue out, and its eyes glaring like marsh fires." "If only the loup-garou were a natural wolf, why then you see," the mayor cleared his throat, "you see we should think nothing of it; but it is a fiend, a worse-than-fiend, a man-wolf-fiend."

Sabine decided to take his chance and walked back to his lodgings and his family. But, he adds, not without picking up a stout stick to fend-off an attack.

The War on Wolves

Fear of wolves has led people to declare war on the animal. Wolves have been hunted almost to extinction in many parts of the world. During the mid and late nineteenth century, professional wolf hunters such as Dick Brown in Montana USA were responsible for wiping out most of the wolves in the USA. Their methods are still in use today – and they are horrific.

Trapping Wolves

The usual method of trapping wolves is by means of the leg-hold trap. This consists of a steel pan which, when the wolf steps on it to take the bait, is trapped by two steel-pointed jaws which close around the animal's leg. The poor animal now has to wait for the trapper to arrive before his sufferings are at an end and this can be several hours or even several days. In the meantime the wolf makes frantic efforts to escape, pulling and tearing at the trap. Sometimes the animal becomes so demented that it gnaws off its own foot.

In the poster opposite, Montana hunters are warned that wolves are a protected species.

HUNTERS
HAVE YOU SEEN?

2-5 feet tall
5-6 feet long
80-100 pounds
long low howl

life-size track

The Montana Dept. F.W.P. US Forest Service and US Fish & Wildlife Service request that hunters report any sightings or signs of wolves. Information provided by hunters will aid in managing and eventually removing wolves from the endangered species list.

Wolves are protected by State and Federal law under the Endangered Species Act.

Sportsmen Know Your Target before shooting.

Please report any game violations or wolf sightings to Montana Dept. F.W.P. US Forest Service.
Or call USFWS 406 448 5225.

Never Cry Wolf

A young Canadian naturalist, Farley Mowat, studied the habits of the wolf in the Arctic, during the 1950s. He based a book on his life alone with the wolves which he called *Never Cry Wolf.* When he first heard of his assignment he was more than a little alarmed. News was coming in that, in Canada's desolate barren lands, ferocious and hungry wolves were ravaging the deer population. So serious was the problem that the Canadian government had decided to investigate the matter – and Farley Mowat was the man for the mission impossible. He was to live alone amongst the wolves.

He spent several months in the wilderness getting to know the wolves so well as individuals that he gave each one of them a name. What he discovered changed his whole view of wolves. Far from being the vicious and blood-thirsty creatures of his nightmares; he found them to be playful, caring and loyal. The real culprits were the human hunters who were slaughtering the deer by the thousand.

In one dramatic passage from his book he describes his shame at discovering his own irrational fears about wolves. He had studied the animals all summer and they had got used to him. As his assignment drew to a close and winter approached he decided to take a last close look at the wolf's den. Crawling down the tunnel he came face to face with two wolves, their amber eyes glowing in his torchlight.

'Despite my close familiarity with these wolves, whom I had come to know and respect as friends… deeply ingrained prejudices overmastered reason and experience. I was so frightened that paralysis gripped me.

The wolves did not even growl.'

Mowat then wiggled in retreat back up the tunnel and admitted to himself, *'If I had brought my rifle I might have reacted in brute fury and tried to kill both wolves... Mine had been the fury of resentment born of fear: resentment against the beasts who had engendered terror in me.'*

King of the Wolves

Stories of wolves taking care of infant humans stretch back far into the past.

A Turkish legend tells how their ancestors had been slaughtered in battle. Even women and children had been put to the sword. Miraculously, however, amongst all the dead bodies that littered the battlefield one infant boy, who had been thrown in a nearby marsh to drown, was discovered by a she-wolf. The child wailed and screamed for he was ravenously hungry and the she-wolf, who had lost her cubs to hunters, took pity on the helpless infant.

The child grew big and strong for the mother-wolf fed him constantly and taught him how to hunt with the pack for his own food. The story has it that he joined forces with a she-wolf and produced ten strapping sons. Amongst the litter was one wolf-boy who emerged stronger than the rest and fastest at the hunt.

He soon began to gather human followers who admired the warrior for his prowess in battle. There was no one who would face him in a fight let, alone defeat him, and so his followers begged him to become their king – the very first king of Turkestan.

Saintly Wolf

This story is shrouded in Irish mystery.

Albeus was a sickly boy who was born in fifth century Ireland. Now, it was usual, if the parents thought a baby had little chance of living, to abandon it to die of starvation or be killed by animals. They hadn't reckoned, however, on the love and devotion of a she-wolf who found the little mite and suckled him with her milk.

When little Albeus was a few years old he was discovered by a monk who took him to a nearby monastery and brought him up a Christian. Albeus so impressed the monks with his goodness that he was offered a priesthood.

The story goes that the very same she-wolf that had rescued Albeus was being pursued by hunters and ran into his church to escape the hunters who were in hot pursuit. Albeus stopped them in their tracks and forbade them to enter his church for, as he explained, the animal had the right of sanctuary and no killing was to take place in a sacred place.

Well, it must have been love at first sight for Albeus kept and protected the wolf. When cubs were born they were even made welcome at saintly Albeus' table!

Gone to the Dogs!

In May 1997 the Russian police brought six-year-old Ivan Mishukov to a children's home in Retova, west of Moscow. He was filthy, covered with lice and sores and very violent.

Poor Ivan had led a terrible life, despite his tender age. His father Mikhail had been sent to prison and his mother took a boyfriend who got so drunk every night that he beat the child. His mother lost all interest in him and stopped giving him food.

Mikhail began to scavenge in dustbins and rubbish tips and managed to scrape enough to eat. He often did so in the company of a pack of stray dogs – until he felt more at home with them than with humans. "I was better off with the dogs," he said. "They loved and protected me." Ivan begged for food which he shared with the dogs. At night when the temperatures dropped to minus thirty, they

helped him to find shelter by finding doorways and warm places to sleep where they could cuddle up together. If strangers came too close the dogs snarled to send them off.

When the police tried to 'rescue' Ivan, the dogs went for them, snarling and snapping. The police feared that the dogs might carry the rabies virus and didn't want to take any chances. Eventually they laid a trap for the dogs, by placing bait inside an empty house. Waiting patiently until all the dogs had entered the building they swung the door closed and trapped them inside. Ivan was dragged to safety, kicking, scratching and biting.

The authorities tried to provide Ivan with a settled normal life. He was enrolled at school and looked after at an orphanage with the hope that there might be a family who would want to adopt him.

In the Company of Wolves

Misha was only seven in 1940 when the Germans overran Belgium where she lived. Her Jewish parents were arrested and she never saw them again. At first she was hidden in a neighbour's house but she grew afraid that she might be handed over to the Germans, so she ran away in the hope that she might find her parents. Travelling by night, she headed for Germany, where she knew her parents had been taken.

One night, as she made her way through a forest, she tripped and twisted her ankle. The pain was so intense that she began to howl. A female wolf heard the sounds of the child in distress and padded her way to the source of the sound. She at once took pity on the infant and brought her food. The girl and the wolf soon became good friends, travelling together and even being joined later by a male wolf.

Sadly for Misha, both wolves were eventually killed by hunters and she had to continue her journey alone until she arrived in eastern Poland where she joined another wolf pack. When the war ended she walked out of the woods and back to civilisation. Misha left for America and now lives in a quiet Boston suburb with her husband where she wrote about her adventures in the company of wolves – *Misha: A Memoir of the Holocaust Years*.

The Wolf Children of India

A Place of Spirits

The Reverend J. A. L. Singh shook his head and sighed. There was no doubt about it. The villagers were terrified. He listened patiently to their stories of ghosts that hid beneath the canopy of branches and leaves of the jungle. In daylight the undergrowth moved without cause, they complained, and the people felt eyes burning into their backs when they ventured out. They spoke of man-beasts with human form and the head of a devilish animal.

The year was 1920 and the Reverend Singh was making a tour of the villages of the Santal people who lived in a remote part of Bengal, India.

A Strange Discovery

The Reverend was determined to put an end to such superstitious nonsense. He set off to track down these so-called devils and confront them in their lair. Feeling protected by his God, he tracked the creatures to a huge white ant mound. This had been abandoned by the insects and taken over by a she-wolf and her cubs. They'd hollowed out the base with their paws and now occupied it as their den.

Waiting patiently in the long grass, far enough away for his scent not to carry, he watched the wolves came out of their den to sun themselves. It was then that he received the shock of his life. Two of the creatures were strange in shape and appearance. They did not look like animals, even though they behaved as if they were. The hair on their heads was thickly matted and their skins were caked with dirt. They were human! Human children reared and protected by a mother wolf.

The Reverend Singh hatched a plan to rescue the infants but he needed help. His scheme was simple, He would wait until the mother-wolf went off in search of food for her brood then he and the villagers would snatch the children and take them to 'safety'.

The plan sadly misfired for the she-wolf returned too soon and found her off-spring under 'attack'. She snarled and sprang to their defence only to be stabbed through the heart with a spear wielded by one of the villagers.

Without fear of further attack, the men cut through the white ant mound and uncovered a hollowed-out lair in which nestled two wolf cubs and the two human children

which they could see were girls. The two children were taken back to an orphanage run by the Reverend Singh at Midnapore. In their new home they were christened Kamala (meaning 'Lotus') and Amala (meaning 'bright yellow flower').

The Wolf runs Deep

Despite the similarity of their new names the girls were not twins and probably not even related by blood. Bathed and combed they began to look more human but this was only skin deep. Their behaviour was deeply strange and disturbing. They refused to stand upright and even when helped they seemed incapable of straightening their limbs. Neither of the girls would accept anything to drink but milk until, one day, the younger girl, Amala, broke away from her new guardian and fought one of the orphanage dogs for a bone. Victorious in the fight that followed she dragged it to a corner of the yard and gnawed at the strings of remaining flesh. The children refused all cooked meat and would only eat raw flesh.

Another strange eating habit was their desire to swallow earth and stones before passing excrement. Doctor friends of the Reverend Singh explained that they had seen animals do that, for it was the way wolves cleaned their gut of worms.

The two girls also showed odd sleep patterns. They dozed rather than slept deeply. Around midnight they would wake and prowl around the orphanage, occasionally letting out a wolf-like howl. They urinated wherever they were and had no notion of using the toilet. Sometimes they dragged their bottoms along the ground, more from the irritation caused by worms than in an attempt to make themselves clean. Cold weather did not seem to bother them and they would scamper around the yard of the orphanage in all weathers. They did not seem to enjoy the company of people, preferring to roam with the dogs in the compound. Their only friends were the orphanage dogs and the wolf cubs who had been their playmates as children.

The Reverend Singh found it depressingly slow trying to educate them in human ways. Given toys they chewed them up. Approached by other children they growled, snarled at them and scratched. Amala, the youngest girl, aged about three, made the better progress, but this was cut short when she caught a kidney infection from which she died in September 1921.

Slow Beginnings

Now all alone, Kamala began to kneel and slowly stand up, but only in response to food. The animal within her was never far away. Whilst walking with the Reverend Singh in the fields one day her eye caught sight of a flock of vultures tearing at the rotting carcass of a dead cow. The girl dashed from his side on all fours, chased the vultures away and started ripping at the dead animal with her teeth. Reverend Singh, shocked that he'd had so little effect on her behaviour, had to drag her away.

Kamala finally stood up straight one day but only when offered a tasty piece of raw meat. She did not live long enough to develop further human characteristics. Like Amala, Kamala died of kidney failure, perhaps as a result of poisoning from her bizarre eating habits.

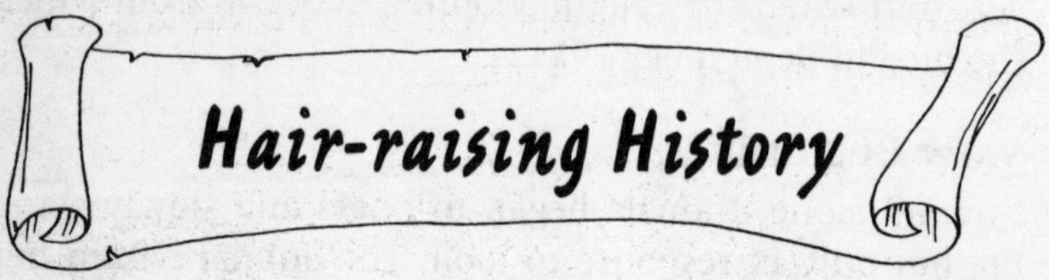

Amala and Kamala were not the only children in India to be discovered being reared by wolves. In this story a young boy-wolf is found.

Wolf-boy

Narsingh Singh was lost in his own thoughts as he bicycled through the great stretch of forest near his home town in the region of Uttar Pradesh, India. He owned a number of scattered fields and had just finished inspecting them. All was well. It would be a good harvest this year. Enough to earn him a new bicycle that was long overdue.

And so he would have continued, unmindful of the ruts and ribbons of mud that passed as tracks through the heart of the forest, if a rustle in the undergrowth had not made him stop. He peered cautiously into the tangle of undergrowth. "Careful,"' he thought to himself. "A wounded animal is the most dangerous." He had nothing that he could use to protect himself. He searched the muddy track, looking for a knotted branch to act as a club but could only find a large stone. Balancing the rock in his hand, ready to fling it at whatever was there, he stepped forward gingerly.

Discovery

Parting the bush near the track he saw four or five wolf cubs playing rough and tumble. In the middle of the tiny yelping pack of tumbling fur and tails there appeared to be a human child about four or five years old. Narsingh's eyes quickly scanned for the she-wolf but he could see no evidence of the fearsome mother.

Dashing forward he swept the child up into his arms. The boy struggled furiously, scratching Narsingh with his talons. His open mouth snapped backwards and forwards trying to bite this enemy who had interrupted his game. Carrying the child to his bicycle, Narsingh wrapped the boy tightly in a cotton towel and strapped him to the crossbar of the bike.

After a struggle, Narsingh managed to get the boy home where he adopted him and named him Shamadeo. The boy showed every sign of having being reared by wolves. He could not stand erect but ran on all fours. The skin on his palms, elbows and knees was hardened like the pads of a wolf's paws and his hair was filthy and matted.

His teeth were uneven and pointed, his nails were more like claws, and his eyes glittered a luminous yellow. He could utter only the most horrible snarls and howls, and ran to play with the dogs whenever he could. At night he had to be tied up for fear that he would run out and hunt with the jackals that seemed to call to him. Most disturbing of all, he had a yearning for raw meat. On one terrible occasion, horrified villagers watched as he attacked a chicken, ripping it apart and tearing out its innards.

Wolf-boy Abandoned

Some of the villagers questioned Narsingh's motives for rescuing the child. He had rescued a child once before – a small boy thrown by its mother into a drain when barely born. The child, named Ramadeo, had grown up mentally weak but, as Narsingh pointed out, was still capable of working as a labourer on his farm. Village gossips said Narsingh had taken advantage of Ramadeo and was doing the same thing with Shamadeo. Rumours spread that he was charging curious visitors to gawp at the wolf-boy.

Shamadeo made little progress. He never learned to speak but did learn to sign a few words to make himself understood. With constant massaging of his legs he eventually straightened his limbs and learned to walk upright and within three years he was doing odd jobs such as looking after Narsingh's cows. Slowly, he was weaned off raw meat, but he still tried to eat dirt and earth. Eventually, with patience, he began to eat the same food as his adopted family.

Wolf-boy's Final Days

What happened next is shrouded in mystery. Shamadeo either left or was driven away from Narsingh's family. No one really knows why but he was found alone and

starving by a group of nuns. Taking pity on the boy they placed him in one of Mother Theresa's Homes for the Destitute and Dying in the city of Lucknow. He lived there for the remaining seven years of his life.

The nuns gave him a new name – Pascal, and tried to teach him to read and write. But he learned little and the nuns shook their heads when the boy continually sought out dogs to play with. He never trusted the other children who lived in constant fear of an attack from him.

He died at the home in 1985 after a terrible attack of cramps which the nuns found impossible to treat or to ease. Photographs taken shortly after his death show him to have wasted away to little more than skin stretched over a thin framework of bones.

What was the Truth about the Wolf-children?

Not everyone believes the story of the Indian wolf children. In both cases it has been suggested that the children may have suffered from a disorder called 'autism'. People who have autism find it very difficult to communicate normally. Probably their parents, too poor to afford to keep them, abandoned them in the forest. We have only the word of the two men that they were discovered in the company of wolves. Narsingh was accused of making money from exhibiting the wolf-boy and the Reverend Singh of trying to attract money for his orphanage.

Whilst some of this may be true it does not explain why the children ran on all fours and would only eat raw meat. Perhaps in some way they had learned this behaviour from animals.

Werewolves

As we have seen, wolves are not nightmare creatures but animals that display many good qualities – even looking after human children abandoned by their parents. A werewolf, on the other hand, is a human who changes into the form of a wolf to satisfy a need to taste human flesh or at least, that is the explanation humans have come up with, because what other explanation could there be for such bizarre behaviour? How else would it be possible to explain a human turning against its own kind and devouring human flesh?

Modern Werewolf Stories

Unfortunately these are a lot more common than you might imagine. Check the newspapers!

The Strange Case of Mr X

In 1988 a group of psychologists from the Bordeaux prison service in France reported the bizarre case of a prisoner who claimed he was a werewolf. Being unable to reveal his true name the doctors simply referred to him as Mr X.

His story, at first glance, seemed typical of that of a violent criminal but as they investigated further it took on some odd facts. 'X' was a tough-looking character – bulging muscles, deep-set staring eyes and his face and heavily tattooed arms criss-crossed with scars. He had been put away for a very violent assault in which his victim had died. Sadly, there was nothing too out of the ordinary in this – the prisons were full of such misfits, usually victims of unhappy, violent childhoods themselves. And 'X' had a string of convictions for violent attacks.

It was not until they interviewed 'X', however, that they were startled out of the humdrum world of the criminal into the frontiers of insanity and superstition. There was an explanation for his behaviour, he announced to his startled listeners, for he had been for many years – a werewolf!

"It is when I make myself bite like a rabid dog... as soon as I see blood I want to swallow it, to drink it... if I happen to cut myself, I drink my own blood... when I suffer an emotional shock, I feel myself undergoing a transformation, it's like my fingers are paralysed, I get a feeling like ants crawling in the middle of my hand, I am

no longer master of myself... I have the impression of becoming a wolf, I look at myself in the mirror, I see myself transforming, it's absolutely no longer my own face changing, the eyes stare out, wild-looking, the pupils dilate, I feel as if hairs are bristling out all over me, as if my teeth are growing longer and afterwards I lose consciousness."

He went on to describe his craving for blood to the stunned doctors. In order to satisfy this bizarre need he would visit slaughter-houses and drink the warm blood of horses but, "it isn't animal blood I prefer, but human blood".

Prison doctors had heard many stange tales in their professional careers. Sometimes the stories had been made up in the hope that the prisoner might be released or get better treatment, so they decided to check this one out with people who knew him. The first person they interviewed was the 'werewolf's' girlfriend. She told them that 'X' often howled like a wolf at night and slept only lightly like an animal afraid of attack. She also confirmed that her boyfriend flew into violent rages and tried to bite anyone who came near him.

But did he really believe he was a werewolf? Was he suffering from lycanthropy? The doctors questioned more of his friends and also members of his family. They told the doctors that you could rarely believe 'X' about anything as he told such outrageous lies. Certainly he had told some huge whoppers about his own childhood. But there was enough evidence to confirm that he'd had a hard early life. And his girlfriend was quite convinced of his strange wolf-like behaviour – enough to suggest that 'X' believed himself to be a werewolf.

In their attempt to put a name to 'X's' illness the doctors came up with 'mythomania' – 'a voluntary and conscious need to lie where the behaviour is out of the patient's control'. In other words, 'X' had lied to himself so well that he had convinced himself that he really was a werewolf! So next time you tell a fib just look into the mirror. Notice anything happening? Hair today, goon tomorrow!

Investigating Werewolves

Many doctors today are reluctant to diagnose their patients as suffering from lycanthropy, regarding the term as old-fashioned or irrelevant. There are also fewer cases of patients who believe themselves to have transformed into animals, probably as a result of more people living in towns, far from contact with wild animals. Other cases reported by doctors have largely been a result of drug abuse, such as the following case of Mr H.

Doctors Surawicz and Banta described two cases of lycanthropy in 1975. One concerned a Mr H who had taken LSD whilst living in the woods alone. Under the influence of the drug he felt he was turning into a werewolf with fur bursting from his hands and face. He felt a desperate desire to chase rabbits and kill them for food. The doctors could do nothing for him for his mind had become permanently damaged.

The second case involved a farmer, referred to in the doctors' reports as Mr W. He had lived on his own for so long that he had developed some strange habits. He'd allowed his hair and beard to grow uncontrolled so that they had both become a thick, tangled and greasy mass. When a full moon appeared he would howl and he had taken to sleeping in cemeteries.

Mr W was convinced that he had become a werewolf. The doctors, however, discovered a different explanation. After a brain scan it was discovered that Mr W was suffering from a brain disease. His werewolf delusions were treated with drugs and he was able to continue a more or less normal life.

The Werewolf Lives On!

Cases of patients who believe themselves to be werewolves usually have a common-sense explanation such as disturbed childhoods, hallucinations from drugs or brain disease. What is surprising, however, is the persistence of the werewolf – at least in our imaginations! And it is this that Hollywood feeds on. The first werewolf movies appeared in the 1930s with *The Werewolf of London* and *The Wolf Man* but they never caught on as much as the vampire films. Vampires and werewolves were brought together for a double-starring role in *Return of the Vampire,* and strictly for laughs by two comedians in *Abbott and*

Costello Meet Frankenstein. In this movie, Wolf Man joins the comedians in an attempt to prevent Dracula from transplanting Abbott's brain into that of Frankenstein. Or you could watch out for *I was a Teenage Werewolf*.

Tail-Piece

Have you survived all these hair-raising stories about werewolves? Are you worried that someone you know might be going to the 'dogs'? Do they need to be 'hounded' out of town? Look out for the tell-'tail' signs in the picture below.

Index

Also from Hodder Children's Books

Truly Terrible Tales

Scientists

Writers

Explorers

Inventors

Jack Marlowe
illustrated by Scoular Anderson

History is crammed with amazing stories!
In these four books you can find out all about the terrible but true lives of famous scientists, writers, explorers and inventors through the ages:

Creepy John Dee, Tudor scientist – or wicked magican?

Roman horror king Seneca, whose own death was as nasty as his bloodthirsty plays ...

Fearless Florence Baker, Victorian explorer, who saw her own grave being dug ...

And Ancient Greek Archimedes, creator of the deadly ship-smasher!

Order Form

0 340 73992 4	Truly Monstrous Tales: **Vampires**	£3.99	☐
0 340 73993 2	Truly Monstrous Tales: **Werewolves**	£3.99	☐
0 340 73994 0	Truly Monstrous Tales: **Mummies**	£3.99	☐

All Hodder Children's books are available at your local bookshop or newsagent, or can be ordered direct from the publisher. Just tick the titles you want and fill in the form below. Prices and availability subject to change without notice.

Hodder Children's Books, Cash Sales Department, Bookpoint, 39 Milton Park, Abingdon, Oxon, OX14 4TD, UK. If you have a credit card you may order by telephone – (01235) 400414.

Please enclose a cheque or postal order made payable to Bookpoint Ltd to the value of the cover price and allow the following for postage and packing:

UK & BFPO – £1.00 for the first book, 50p for the second book, and 30p for each additional book ordered, up to a maximum charge of £3.00.

OVERSEAS & EIRE – £2.00 for the first book, £1.00 for the second book, and 50p for each additional book.

Name ....

Address ....

....

....

If you would prefer to pay by credit card, please complete the following:

Please debit my Visa/Access/Diner's Card/American Express (delete as applicable) card no:

---- ---- ---- ---- ---- ---- ---- ---- ---- ---- ---- ---- ---- ---- ---- ----

Signature ....

Expiry Date ....